My Baby Brother and Me

A MEMORY SCRAPBOOK FOR KIDS

written by
JANE DRAKE and ANN LOVE

illustrated by
SCOT RITCHIE

KIDS CAN PRESS

My Baby Brother and Me

My name is _____.

My family's special name for me is _____.

I was born on _____ _____, _____.
                       (month)   *(day)*   *(year)*

I am _____ years old.

I was born in _____, _____.
                     (city/town)   *(country)*

Here's a picture of me:

My baby brother's name is _____.

My special name for him is _____.

He was born on _____ _____, _____.
                     (month)   (day)   (year)

He is _____ old.
      (days, weeks or months)

He was born in _____, _____.
                   (city/town)   (country)

Here's a picture of my baby brother:

Waiting for My Baby Brother

When my parents told me a new baby was coming, I felt

- ☐ happy
- ☐ sad
- ☐ angry
- ☐ proud
- ☐ _____

Before my baby brother arrived, I wanted

- ☐ a brother
- ☐ a sister
- ☐ twins
- ☐ a puppy
- ☐ _____

While I waited for him, I

- ☐ dressed my teddy in baby clothes
- ☐ felt my mother's tummy
- ☐ pretended I was a baby
- ☐ thought about all the things we could do together
- ☐ _____

I asked my parents if

☐ he would be my friend

☐ he would look like me

☐ I had to share my toys with him

☐ we could get a fire engine instead

☐ _____

I got ready for the baby by helping to

☐ decorate his room

☐ collect my baby toys for him

☐ choose new sheets for his crib

☐ sort baby clothes

☐ wash my old car seat

☐ _____

Welcoming My Baby Brother

When I first saw my baby brother, he was *(circle the picture)*

The first time I saw my baby brother, I thought he

⬚ smelled nice   ⬚ was wrinkled

⬚ was small   ⬚ felt soft

⬚ looked cute   ⬚ _____

I wanted to call him _____.

If he was a girl, his name would be _____.

We chose his name because

⬚ I liked it   ⬚ it suited him

⬚ it's a family name   ⬚ _____

On my baby brother's first day home, we had visits from our

☐ grandparents

☐ neighbors

☐ friends

☐ _____

When I held my baby brother, I

☐ sat very still

☐ rocked him gently

☐ smiled for a picture

☐ _____

I felt

☐ happy

☐ worried

☐ proud

☐ _____

The best part of the day was _____.

Our Family Tree

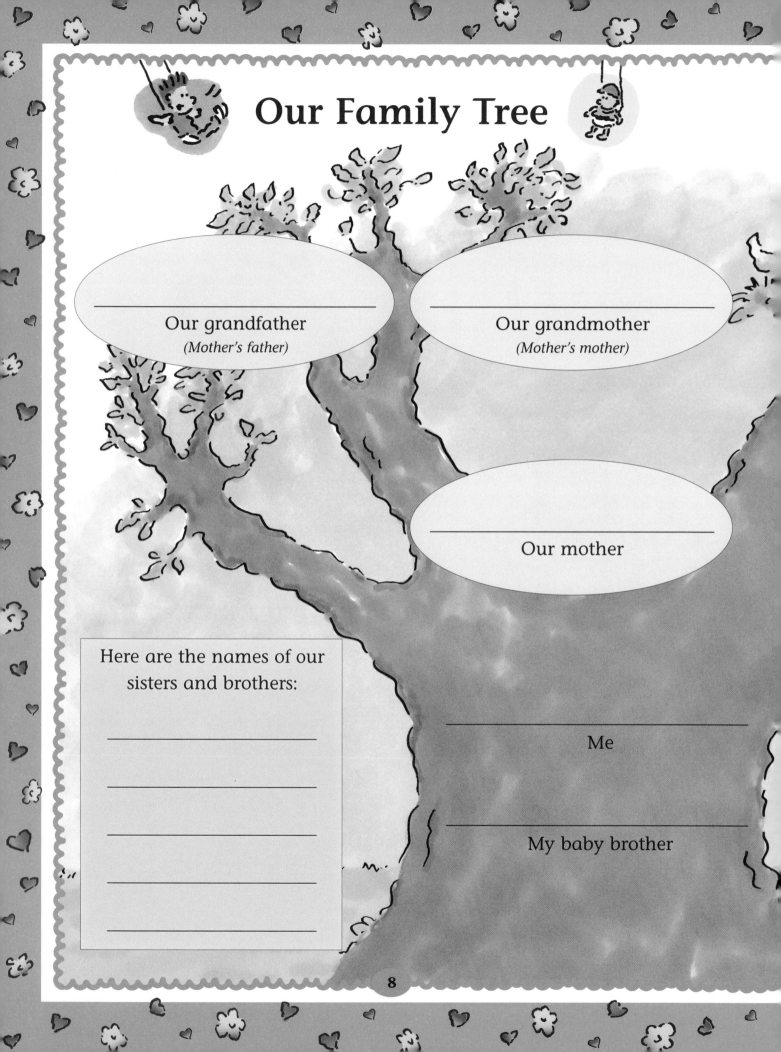

_____
Our grandfather
(Mother's father)

_____
Our grandmother
(Mother's mother)

_____
Our mother

Here are the names of our
sisters and brothers:

_____

_____

_____

_____

_____
Me

_____
My baby brother

_____
Our grandfather
(Father's father)

_____
Our grandmother
(Father's mother)

_____
Our father

Here are the pets
in our family:

_____

_____

_____

_____

_____

Look at Him, Look at Me

Here's a picture of my baby brother and me:

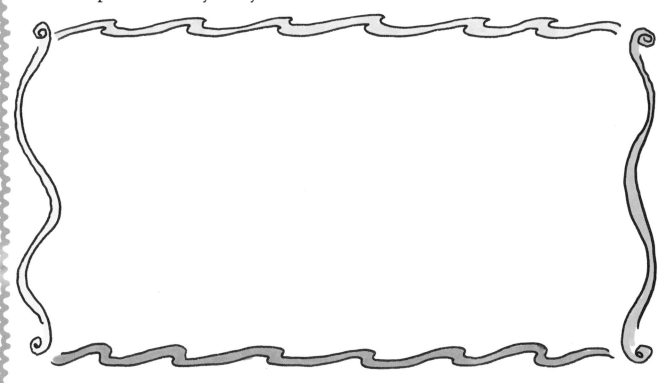

I am _____ tall.   My baby brother is _____ long.

I weigh _____ .   He weighs _____ .

I have _____ teeth.   He has _____ teeth.

I have _____ eyes.   He has _____ eyes.

I have _____ hair.   He has _____ hair.

I have _____ , but my brother doesn't.

Here's a print of my foot:

Here's a print of my baby brother's foot:

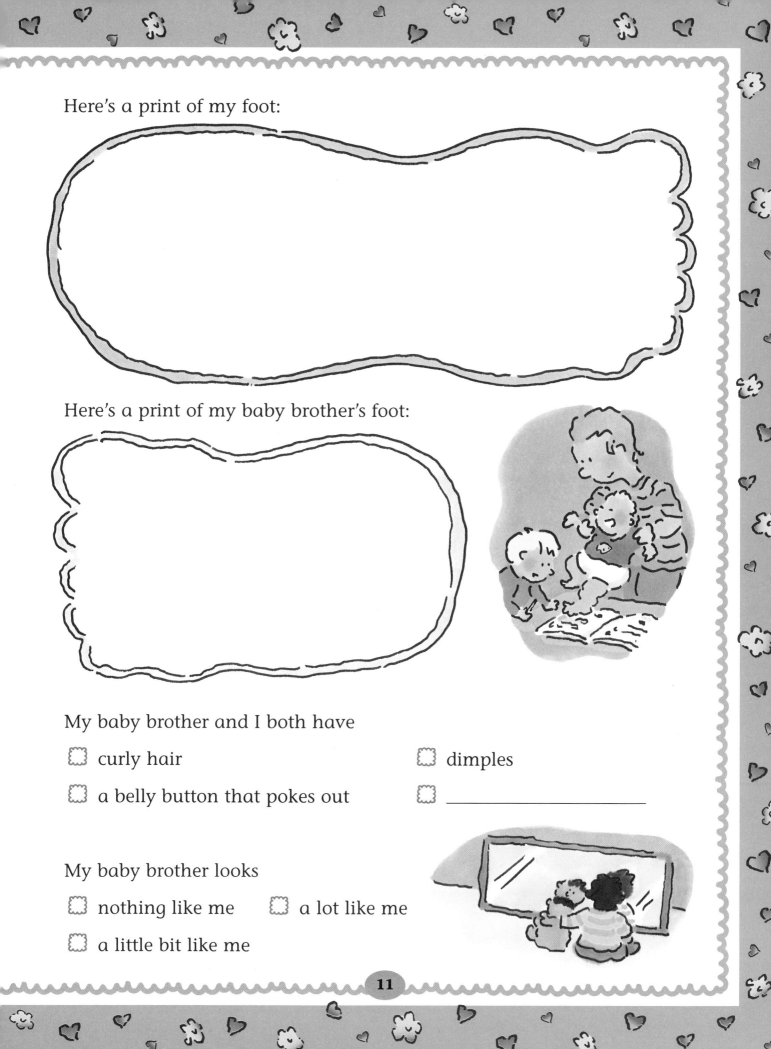

My baby brother and I both have

- [ ] curly hair
- [ ] a belly button that pokes out
- [ ] dimples
- [ ] _____

My baby brother looks

- [ ] nothing like me
- [ ] a lot like me
- [ ] a little bit like me

My Day, His Day

When we are together, my baby brother always

- ☐ fills his diaper
- ☐ holds my finger
- ☐ smiles
- ☐ falls asleep
- ☐ cries
- ☐ _____

My baby brother has _____ naps every day.
(number)

When my baby brother sleeps, my favorite thing to do is *(circle the picture)*

When my baby brother wakes up, we

- ☐ put small toys out of his reach
- ☐ go grocery shopping
- ☐ look at books
- ☐ change his diaper
- ☐ go for a walk
- ☐ _____

Sometimes I leave my baby brother and go to

- ☐ play with friends
- ☐ sleep over at our grandparents'
- ☐ school
- ☐ my music lesson
- ☐ _____

When I get home, my brother is usually *(circle the picture)*

At Home Together

This is where I spend lots of time with my baby brother *(circle the picture):*

I share these things with my baby brother:

☐ bedroom ☐ bath ☐ toys ☐ _____

I don't share my _____ with my baby brother.

I'm not a baby anymore, so I let my brother use my baby things.

Here's what he uses *(circle the pictures):*

There's more work around the house with a baby brother.

I help by

- [ ] getting him a clean diaper
- [ ] burping him
- [ ] playing with him
- [ ] picking up our toys
- [ ] _____

One new chore I don't like is _____.

Because I'm older, sometimes I

- [ ] answer the phone
- [ ] feed our pet
- [ ] read a book by myself
- [ ] bring in the mail
- [ ] dress myself
- [ ] _____

Out and About Together

When we go out, I get around like this *(circle the pictures)*:

My baby brother gets around like this *(circle the pictures)*:

We like walking to

☐ the park ☐ my school

☐ the store ☐ _____

My baby brother gets excited when he sees

☐ airplanes ☐ buses

☐ birds ☐ _____

Here are some special things I collected when we were out together:

Time to Eat

I eat _____ meals a day.
(number)

Here are some of the things I like to eat (circle the pictures):

I eat with

☐ a spoon   ☐ chopsticks

☐ a fork   ☐ _____

Sometimes my food goes

☐ in the air

☐ on my clothes

☐ into the dog's mouth

☐ _____

After I eat, I

☐ help clear the table   ☐ go and play

☐ wash my face and hands   ☐ _____

18

My baby brother eats _____ meals a day.
(number)

Here's what he eats (circle the pictures):

I think my baby brother's food looks

☐ yucky

☐ yummy

☐ _____

My baby brother eats with

☐ my mother's help   ☐ his fingers

☐ my help   ☐ _____

After he eats, he

☐ needs to be burped

☐ sleeps

☐ needs clean clothes

☐ _____

 # Time for Bed

Before my baby brother goes to bed, I always

- [ ] say "good night, sleep tight"
- [ ] sing him a lullaby
- [ ] cuddle him
- [ ] rock him gently
- [ ] turn on his mobile
- [ ] _____

This is what my brother takes to bed:

- [ ] his rattle
- [ ] his fuzzy bunny
- [ ] his soother
- [ ] _____

When my brother cries in the night, I

- [ ] plug my ears
- [ ] get my father
- [ ] give him his favorite toy
- [ ] don't hear him
- [ ] _____

Before I go to bed, I need

- ☐ a drink
- ☐ a hug
- ☐ a story
- ☐ the night light turned on
- ☐ _____

This is what I always take to bed:

- ☐ my favorite book
- ☐ my special blanket
- ☐ my cat
- ☐ _____

When I wake up, I usually hear

- ☐ my baby brother crying
- ☐ my baby brother gurgling
- ☐ my mother talking to my baby brother
- ☐ _____

 # When We Laugh

My baby brother makes me laugh when he

☐ pees while his diaper is being changed

☐ throws his bottle

☐ puts his bowl on his head

☐ gets the hiccups

☐ _____

My baby brother doesn't talk, but he makes these funny noises:

☐ "ga-ga-ga"   ☐ "wa-wa-wa"

☐ "mom-mom-mom"   ☐ _____

My brother can be very silly. Here's a picture of the silliest face he has ever made:

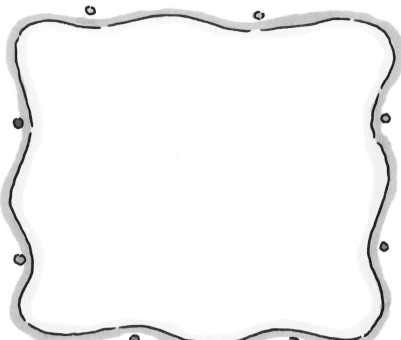

Here's what I do to make my baby brother laugh:

- ☐ play peek-a-boo
- ☐ play pat-a-cake
- ☐ tickle his toes
- ☐ put on a puppet show
- ☐ _____

My baby brother laughs when I say

- ☐ "fuzzy bunny"
- ☐ "goo-goo head"
- ☐ "banana-nana"
- ☐ _____

I can be very silly, too.
Here's a picture of the silliest
face I have ever made:

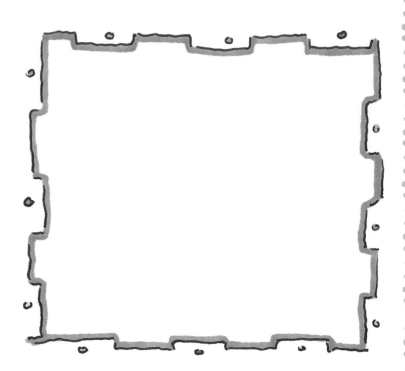

 # When We Cry

Sometimes I feel sad when

- 🔲 my mother feeds my baby brother
- 🔲 my parents tell me to "shhhhh"
- 🔲 my baby brother gets presents and I don't
- 🔲 visitors make a big fuss over my baby brother
- 🔲 _____

I cry when

- 🔲 I hurt myself
- 🔲 I can't find my parents
- 🔲 I have to share my toys
- 🔲 I don't want to go to bed
- 🔲 my parents leave for work
- 🔲 _____

But these things make me feel better (circle the pictures):

My baby brother cries ☐ a lot

☐ sometimes

☐ hardly at all

He cries when he is

☐ teething

☐ tired

☐ hungry

☐ wet

☐ frightened

☐ _____

Here's how we make my baby brother feel better *(circle the pictures)*:

Our Likes and Dislikes

These are my favorite things:

song _____   color _____

game _____   place _____

food _____   book _____

toy _____   animal _____

rhyme _____   friend _____

These are some things I don't like:

☐ the dark

☐ baths

☐ big dogs

☐ nap time

☐ _____

These are my baby brother's favorite things:

song _____   color _____

game _____   place _____

food _____   book _____

toy _____   animal _____

rhyme _____   friend _____

I don't think my brother likes
- mushed carrots
- wet diapers
- being alone
- loud noises
- _____

27

I Can, He Can

I'm big! I can

☐ ride a bike with training wheels

☐ swing by myself

☐ brush my teeth

☐ read a book

☐ reach the cookie jar

☐ _____

I can, but my baby brother can't

☐ play with small toys

☐ sleep in a big bed

☐ use the potty

☐ do up buttons

☐ do a somersault

☐ _____

I am learning to

☐ tie my shoes

☐ zip zippers

☐ brush my hair

☐ make my bed

☐ skate

☐ _____

My baby brother is little, but he can

- ▢ roll over
- ▢ sit up
- ▢ pull himself to stand up
- ▢ feed himself a cracker
- ▢ smile
- ▢ _____

He can, but I can't

- ▢ blow a spit bubble
- ▢ sleep anywhere

- ▢ scream the loudest
- ▢ _____

I am teaching my baby brother how to

- ▢ clap his hands
- ▢ say my name
- ▢ shake his head
- ▢ say "no"
- ▢ play peek-a-boo
- ▢ _____

When We Get Bigger

When I get bigger, I think I will be

- [ ] a teacher
- [ ] a truck driver
- [ ] a famous athlete
- [ ] _____

When my baby brother gets bigger, I think he will be

- [ ] a clown
- [ ] a chef
- [ ] a rock star
- [ ] a father
- [ ] _____

When my baby brother gets bigger, I will

- [ ] teach him the alphabet
- [ ] take him to school
- [ ] teach him to swim
- [ ] let him play with my stuffed animals
- [ ] _____

When we get bigger, these are some of the things my baby brother and I will do together:

- ☐ play soccer
- ☐ go trick-or-treating
- ☐ have our own lemonade stand
- ☐ _____

Some day I hope we will

- ☐ get bunk beds
- ☐ have our own rooms
- ☐ be best friends
- ☐ have a baby sister
- ☐ _____

When we get bigger, I will tell my brother

- ☐ all the things I taught him
- ☐ that he cried a lot
- ☐ how much I love him
- ☐ that I'm glad he's my baby brother
- ☐ _____

Dedicated to our grown-up baby brothers, Will and Ian — J.D. & A.L.
Dedicated to Flyn, my big brother, with love — S.R.

Text © 2000 Jane Drake and Ann Love
Illustrations © 2000 Scot Ritchie

Kids Can Press acknowledges the support of the Government of Canada, through the
BPIDP, for our publishing activity.

Published in Canada by
Kids Can Press Ltd.
29 Birch Avenue
Toronto, ON M4V 1E2

Published in the U.S. by
Kids Can Press Ltd.
2250 Military Road
Tonawanda, NY 14150

www.kidscanpress.com

Edited by Tara Walker
Designed by Julia Naimska

Printed in Hong Kong, China, by Wing King Tong Company Limited

This book is limp sewn with a drawn–on cover.

CM 00 0 9 8 7 6 5 4 3 2

ISBN   1-55074-639-1

Kids Can Press is a Corus™ Entertainment company